This edition published by Parragon Books Ltd in 2017

Parragon Books Ltd
Chartist House
15–17 Trim Street
Bath BA1 1HA, UK
www.parragon.com

© 2017 MARVEL
Marvel.com

ISBN 978-1-4748-7424-3

Printed in China

MARVEL
THOR ™

PaRragon

Bath • New York • Cologne • Melbourne • Delhi
Hong Kong • Shenzhen • Singapore

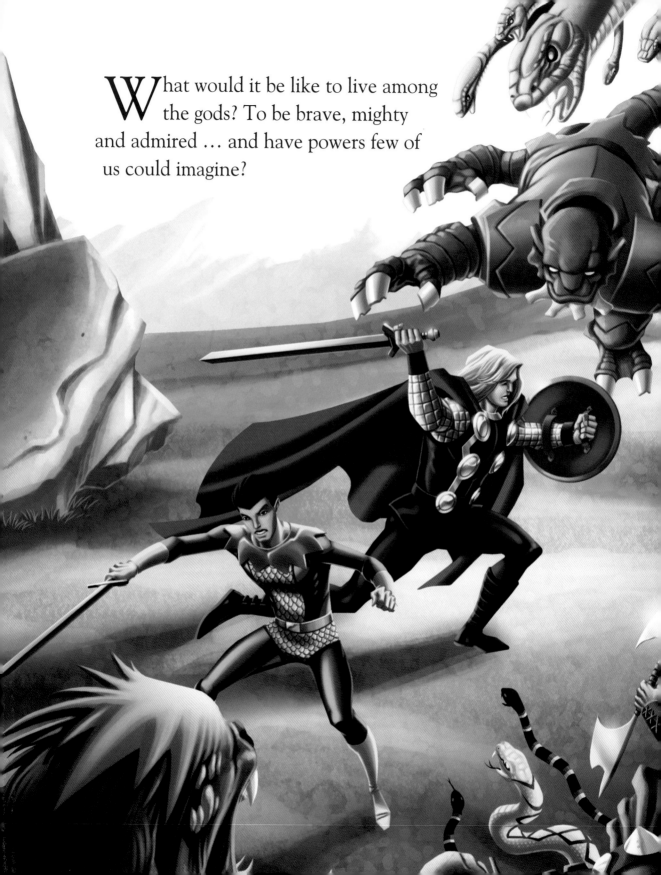

What would it be like to live among the gods? To be brave, mighty and admired … and have powers few of us could imagine?

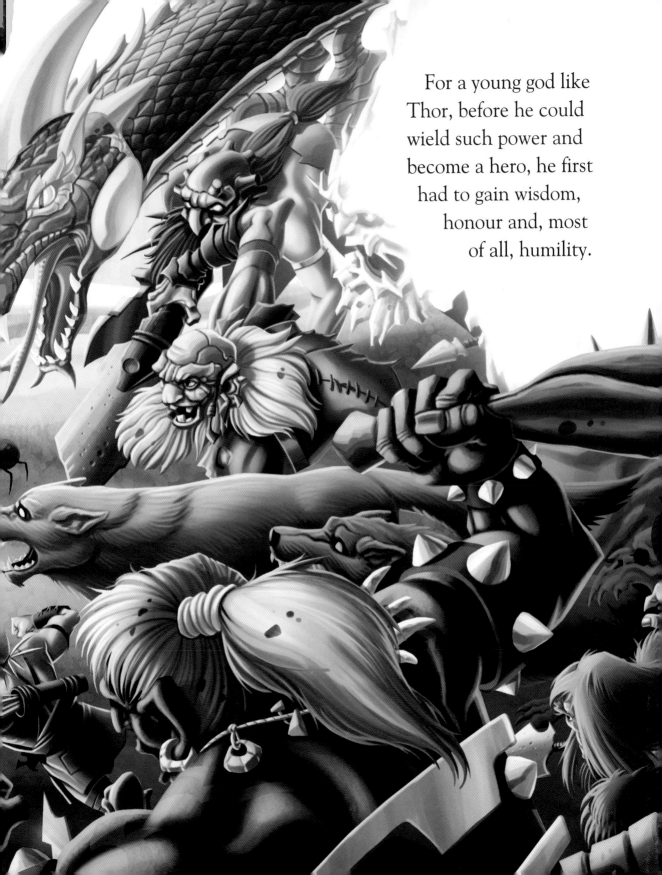

For a young god like
Thor, before he could
wield such power and
become a hero, he first
had to gain wisdom,
honour and, most
of all, humility.

Thor's home was Asgard, a golden realm in the heavens. The Asgardians knew Earth as Midgard. The only way to reach it was across the magnificent Rainbow Bridge, Bifrost. Day and night, the ever-alert Heimdall stood sentry … watchful for threats to Asgard.

As a prince of Asgard, Thor was expected to defend the golden realm when he grew up.

Brash, and a little arrogant, Thor nevertheless chose his friends wisely. He prized loyalty, and the brave warrior Balder, the Warriors Three – Fandral, Volstagg and Hogan – and the valiant Lady Sif were all loyal to a fault.

Thor's father, Odin, and his wife Frigga, wanted nothing more than for Thor to rule Asgard one day, alongside his half-brother Loki.

But while Loki was cunning and clever, there could only be one ruler of Asgard – Thor, the firstborn and rightful heir.

Loki secretly resented the love and affection his parents lavished on Thor, and wanted the throne for himself.

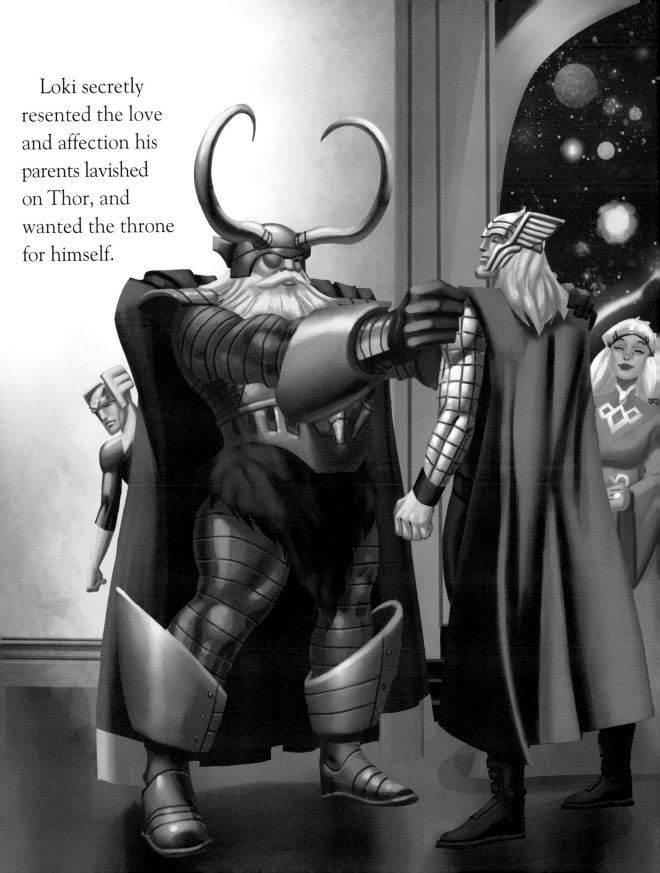

Odin had a powerful and mighty hammer made so that he knew when Thor was ready to rule Asgard. It was forged from a mystical metal called Uru, which came from the heart of a dying star.

The hammer was named Mjolnir.
To claim it, all Thor had to do was lift it off the ground.

But the hammer
was immovable
to Thor.

Thor felt
disappointed. But
the all-father Odin
simply said, "You are
not ready … yet. Be
patient." Loki looked
on, full of resentment.

Proving worthy of Mjolnir became an obsession. As he grew, Thor undertook countless acts of bravery, defending Asgard against Trolls, Frost Giants and other threats.

Thor was honoured by the people of Asgard for acts of nobility.

Thor's noble deeds swiftly became the stuff of legend, and he was admired by his fellow gods.

In battle he was fearless, demonstrating feats of titanic strength. Even the great dragon, Fafnir, was no match for him. Thor also challenged Hela, the Queen of Death, and escaped her icy clutches. "You shall not claim me," he roared.

But it seemed to Thor that, however much he did, it wasn't enough. And still the mystical hammer Mjolnir refused to budge. Every time Thor failed, it brought a smile to Loki's face.

Then, one day …

… Thor finally
proved himself worthy.
The hammer was his.

In no time at all, Thor and Mjolnir were inseparable. Whenever he threw it … the hammer always returned to his hand.

By twirling the hammer,
Thor could soar high
above the ground.

And by slamming it
twice upon the ground …

… he could summon
wind and rain, lightning
and thunder.
    Now he was truly
Thor – God of Thunder.

Odin looked on as Thor's new-found power went to his head, and his arrogance grew. There was still one lesson Thor hadn't learned. And Odin was not happy. In fact, he had grown quite angry with his son.

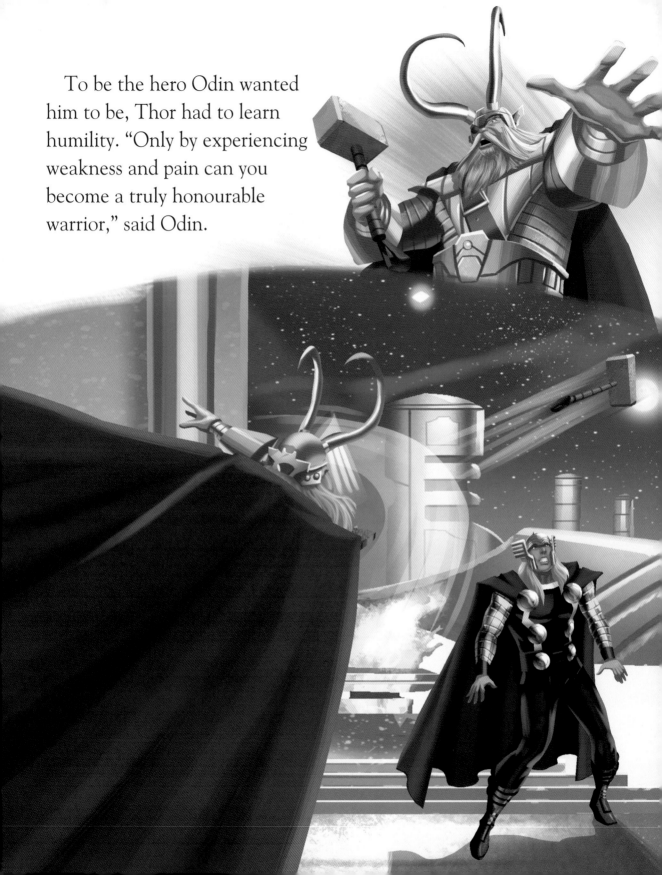

To be the hero Odin wanted him to be, Thor had to learn humility. "Only by experiencing weakness and pain can you become a truly honourable warrior," said Odin.

When Thor rashly defied his father, telling him, "Weakness is for others," Odin snatched Mjolnir from his son's hand and hurled it towards Midgard.

Then, he stripped Thor of his godly armour – and his memory – and sent him to Earth.

Thor awoke in the body of medical student Don Blake, unaware of his true identity.

As Blake, Thor studied hard, harder than he had ever worked in Asgard. Apart from his studies, he also had to cope with the pain of an injured leg. But in the end, he earned his degree.

Blake became a trainee doctor, helping others with illnesses or infirmities. He learned about humanity from his patients, and how they overcame their own weaknesses.

Then, one day, while on holiday in Norway …

… a huge boulder trapped Blake deep underground.
There was no way out.

Using a long wooden stick, he tried to lever a boulder clear of the cave mouth. He struggled, but nothing happened.

Angry at his own weakness, Blake struck the stick on the ground in frustration. There was flash of lightning, a crack of thunder …

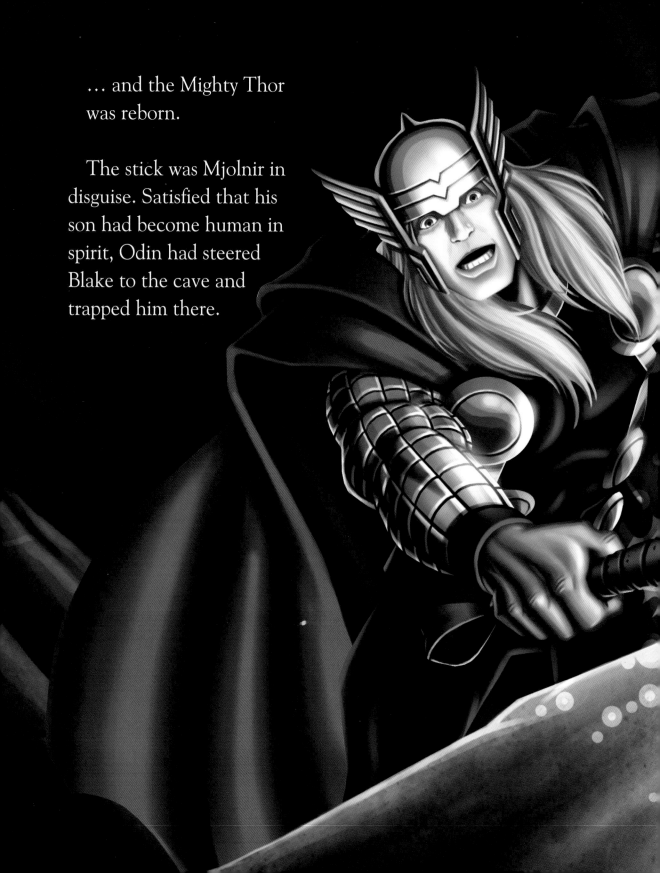

... and the Mighty Thor was reborn.

The stick was Mjolnir in disguise. Satisfied that his son had become human in spirit, Odin had steered Blake to the cave and trapped him there.

His son now had everything
necessary, including humility …

... to become the
hero Asgard – and
Earth – needed.

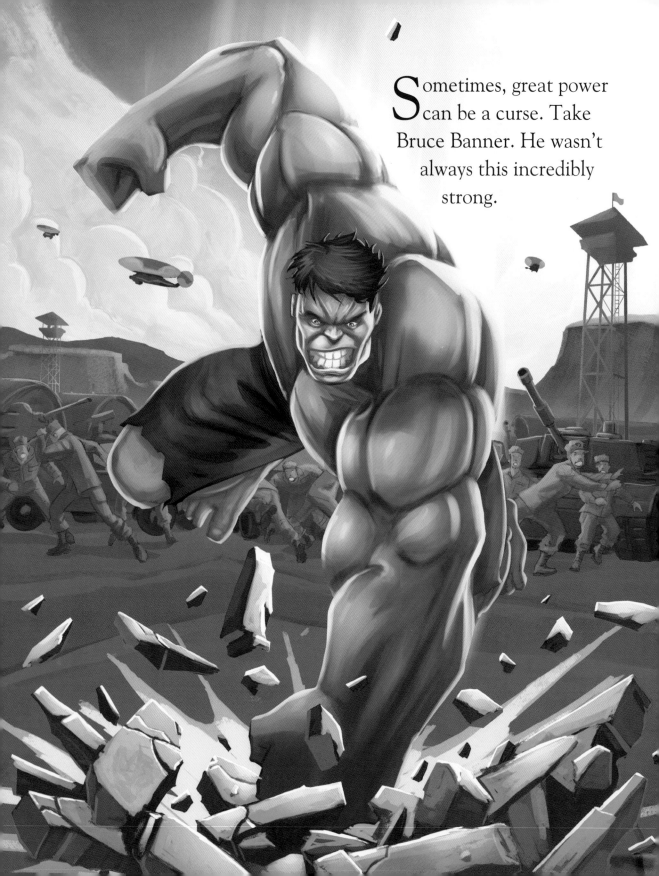

Sometimes, great power can be a curse. Take Bruce Banner. He wasn't always this incredibly strong.

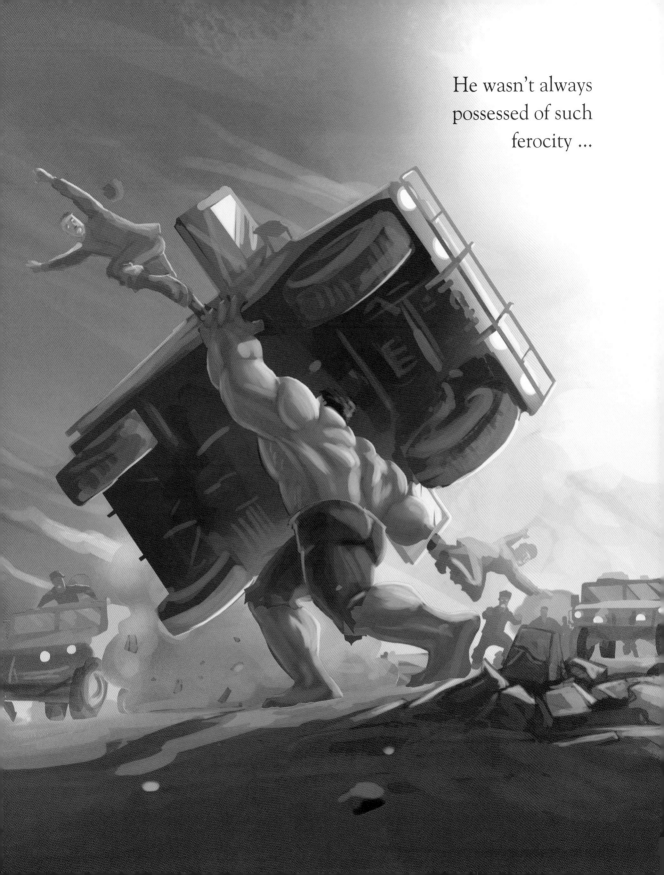

He wasn't always
possessed of such
ferocity ...

... or so full of RAGE!

Once upon a time, such destructive feats as these would have been far beyond his capabilities.

And, more importantly, no one feared him the way they do now.

In fact, it was the other way around. When he was younger Bruce Banner was the scared one.

Bruce was an outsider. He didn't fit in. So often he was sad… and lonely. But even as a child, he was always ready and willing to help someone in need.

As Bruce grew up, he lost himself in books – especially science books. Physics, chemistry, biology – he was endlessly curious about how things worked.

But he never really learned to talk about his feelings, or apply that enquiring mind to the problem of Bruce Banner.

Bruce became a scientist working for the army,
and one of the greatest minds the world had known.

His work on
gamma radiation
was groundbreaking.
He wanted to find
a way to make this
dangerous energy
source a benefit
to mankind.

Bruce felt the only way to fully understand gamma radiation was to create a massive explosion ...

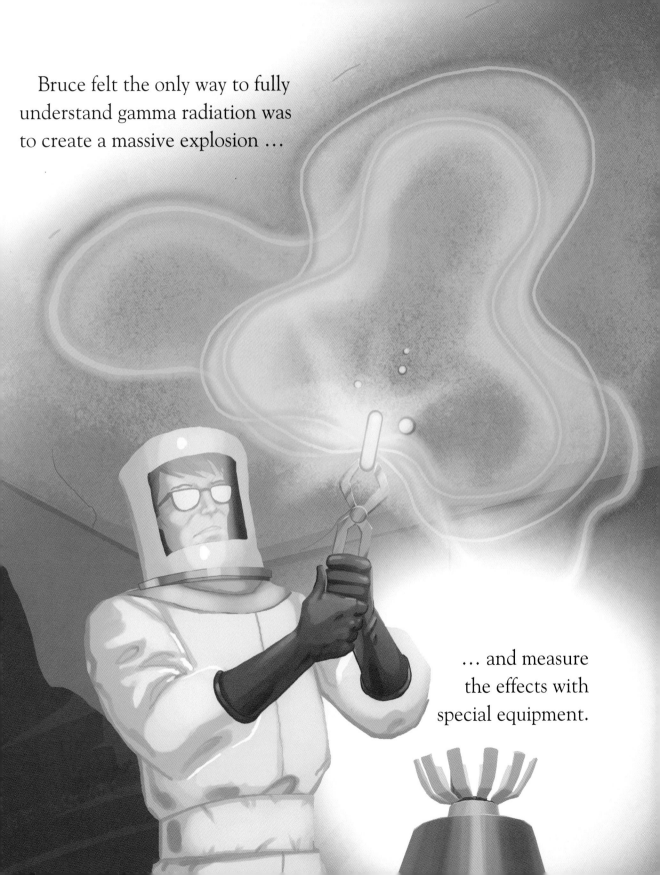

... and measure the effects with special equipment.

Needless to say, the army had other ideas about his scientific research. They wondered if they could build several gamma bombs.

General 'Thunderbolt' Ross felt that Bruce was taking too much time to complete his work. He wanted the tests wrapped up as soon as possible.
When Bruce tried to explain that safety was the most important thing, Ross lost his temper and shouted at Bruce. "Get a move on!" he roared.

Remembering how
his father had shouted
at him, when he was
younger, Bruce got upset.
He moved the gamma
bomb test forward to the
very next day. But Bruce
insisted that the device
be sent to a remote part
of the desert, far from
populated areas.

The countdown began....

Suddenly, the motion-sensitive alarms Bruce had placed around the test area alerted him to a problem.

Someone had just driven right into the danger zone.

Bruce rushed out of the lab. He couldn't let anyone be hurt by his experiment.

Bruce drove out to warn the young man in person. "You have to get clear," he yelled, "before it's too late!"

But it was already too late. With only seconds to act, Bruce propelled the startled teenager into a blast-proof shelter. But the shelter sealed automatically before Bruce could follow him inside.

The teenager, Rick Jones, looked on in horror
as the final seconds ticked away. 5, 4, 3, 2, 1 …

Then Bruce
Banner's world
was torn apart!

But somehow Bruce had survived. No one knew how. It was a miracle. Unfortunately for Bruce … the nightmare was just beginning.

"Doc, you saved my life," Rick said, thanking Bruce over and over. But Bruce wasn't listening.

Deep down, he knew, something had changed inside him. And not for the better!

Bruce felt scared, confused and helpless. It reminded him of his childhood. And the more he thought about the past …

… the angrier he got.

Then Bruce found out just how much the gamma radiation had changed him.

It had turned him into a monster!

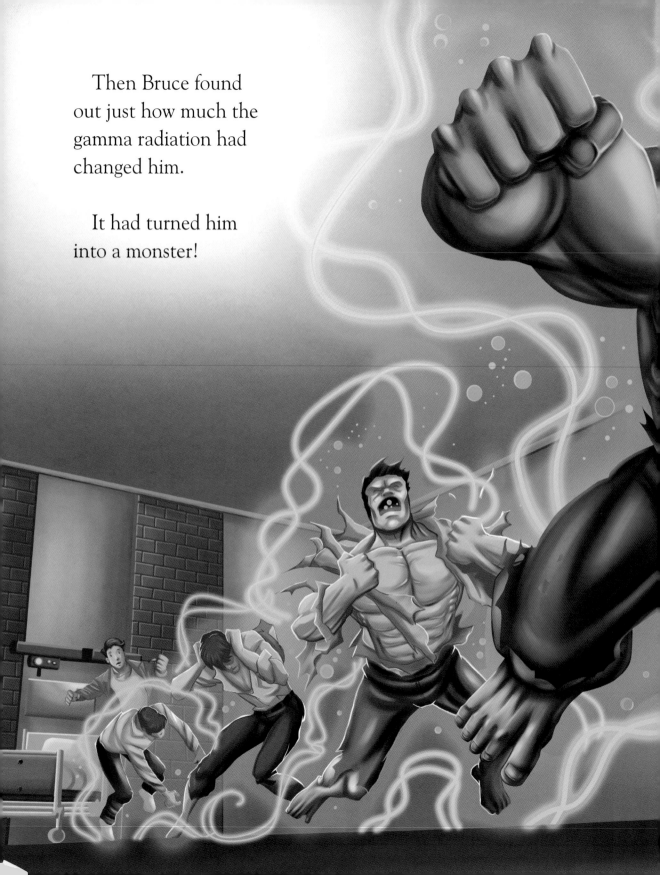

Rick Jones couldn't believe his eyes. "Doc…" he whispered, "what's happened to you?" Even if he'd wanted to, Bruce couldn't have told him. Bruce was gone …

… and in his place stood something terrifying.

"Look at that … hulk," a soldier stammered as the monster burst through the wall of the army hospital. The name stuck. The Incredible Hulk was born.

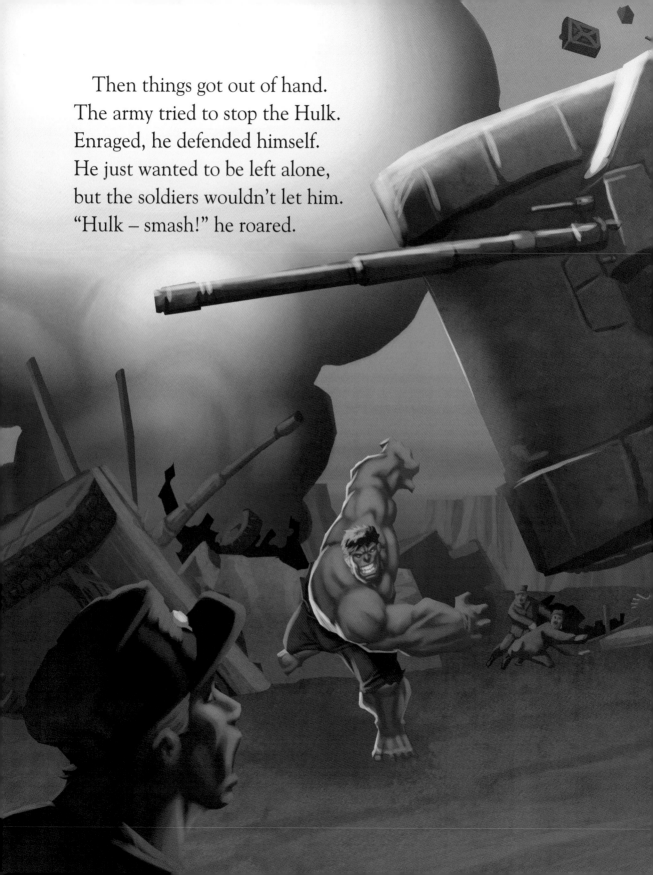

Then things got out of hand.
The army tried to stop the Hulk.
Enraged, he defended himself.
He just wanted to be left alone,
but the soldiers wouldn't let him.
"Hulk – smash!" he roared.

He didn't want
to hurt anyone. But
when he hurled a
tank and it smashed
into a watchtower,
he quickly realized
that the people on
the ground were
in danger.

And enough
of Bruce Banner
remained in the bestial
creature to make
him act.

Using his massively muscled legs, he leaped high into the air and smashed the falling watchtower to splinters.

The Hulk had saved the soldiers that would have been crushed!

But the Hulk didn't want their thanks. He just wanted to be free, and bounded away.

When he had calmed down, the Hulk became Bruce Banner again. But he worried that he could change back at any time.

People could get hurt. And so …

... Bruce Banner thought it best to hide, as far away from other people as possible. This new-found power of his ...

... was a curse he would have to live with, possibly for the rest of his life.